Mummy Cuddles

igloobooks

I love your morning cuddles, Mummy,
especially when you hold me tight and
tickle my tummy to make me giggle.

Mummy, you are wonderful because you bounce around the purple meadow with me and we have so much fun.

I bring you bunches of pretty flowers because they make you smile and you always give me a big cuddle to say thank you.

Mummy, I love it when we look at our
reflections in the forest stream and
pull lots of silly faces together.

When I fall and hurt my paw, you are
always there to give me a big cuddle, wipe
my tears away and kiss it better.

You are the best mummy because you collect big, juicy carrots with me and you never get upset if I eat too many.

When we hop home through the woods, you show me all of the beautiful butterflies, with their wings that flitter-flutter.

You're so much fun, Mummy, because when
I want to burrow in the meadow and get
all messy, you always join in.

You let me play silly games with all of my friends, like when we go tumbling down the grassy, green hills in the daisy fields.

Mummy, I love you because at bedtime
you sing me sweet lullabies, while the clouds
in the sky turn peachy and golden.

When I am very sleepy and close my eyes, you cuddle me and rock me in our cosy burrow, in the soft moonlight.

Your Mummy cuddles are the best cuddles.

I love you, Mummy, because you are the

best Mummy in the world.